To Eric, the adventurer

Copyright © 1992 by Jill Newton

First published in Great Britain by ABC, All Books for Children,
a division of The All Children's Company Ltd,
33 Museum Street, London WC1A 1LD
All rights reserved. No part of this book may be reproduced or
utilized in any form or by any means, electronic or mechanical,
including photocopying and recording, or by any information
storage and retrieval system, without permission in writing
from the Publisher. Inquiries should be addressed to
Lothrop, Lee & Shepard Books, a division of
William Morrow & Company, Inc.,
1350 Avenue of the Americas, New York,
New York 10019

Printed in Hong Kong

First U.S. Edition
1 2 3 4 5 6 7 8 9 10

Library of Congress Cataloging in Publication Data was not
available in time for publication of this book, but can be
obtained from the Library of Congress.
ISBN 0-688-11423-7   ISBN 0-688-11424-5 (lib. bdg.)
L.C. Number 91-42858

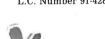

Cat-Fish

Jill Newton

To Kelsey,
on her 5th Birthday

Lothrop, Lee & Shepard Books
New York

Winston was a fisherman's cat. Every night he sat by the fire and listened to tall, fishy tales. The sea sounded much more exciting than the land. Besides, it was filled with his favorite food.

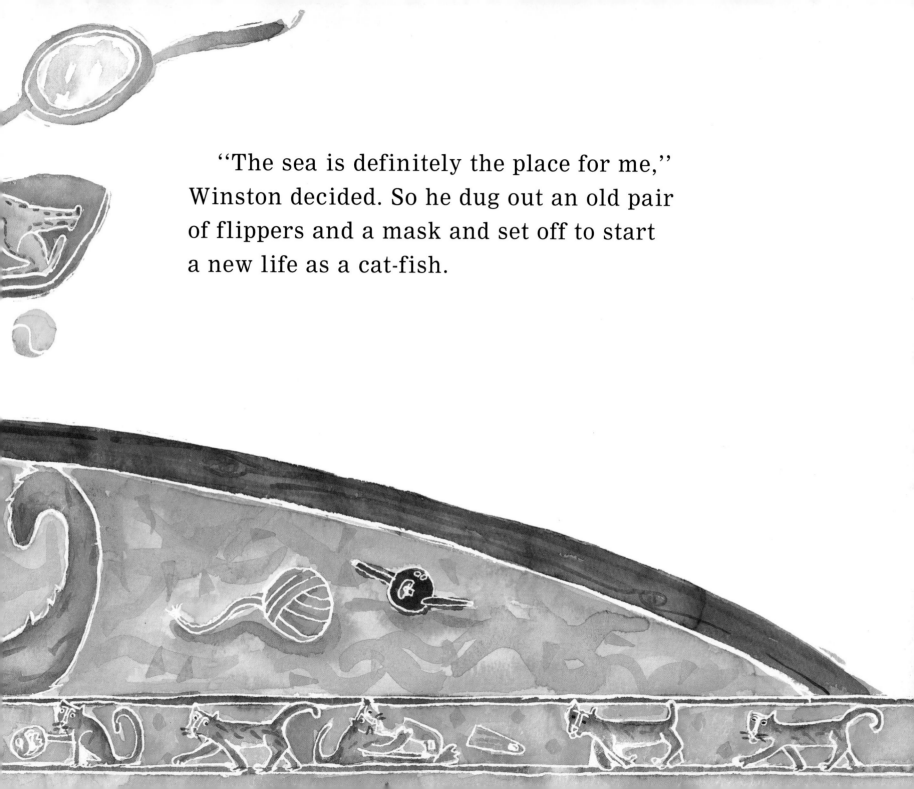

"The sea is definitely the place for me," Winston decided. So he dug out an old pair of flippers and a mask and set off to start a new life as a cat-fish.

The voyage was rough. If he hadn't been so determined, Winston would have changed his mind.

But determined he was. "Now's as good a time as any to begin my adventure," he thought as he was catapulted out of the boat.

"YUCK!" thought Winston. "I forgot about the wet bit. But if fish can cope, so can I. And speaking of fish, I'm starving!"

"Yummy!" he said when a school of fish swam by. Unfortunately, chasing fish proved difficult.

Something appeared to be holding him back.

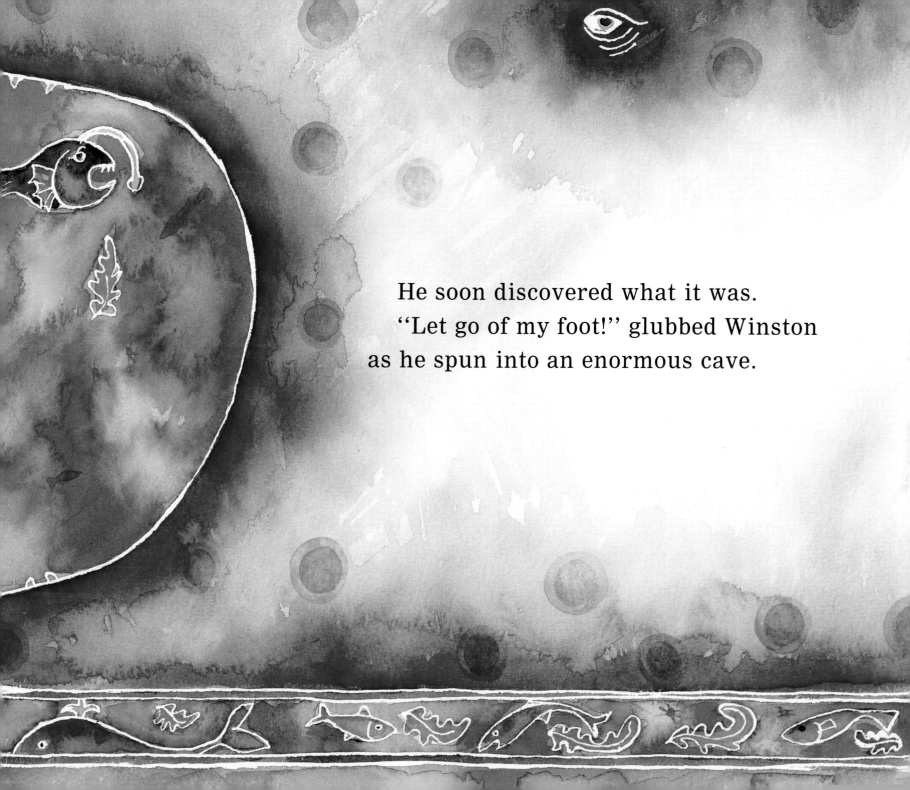

He soon discovered what it was.
"Let go of my foot!" glubbed Winston
as he spun into an enormous cave.

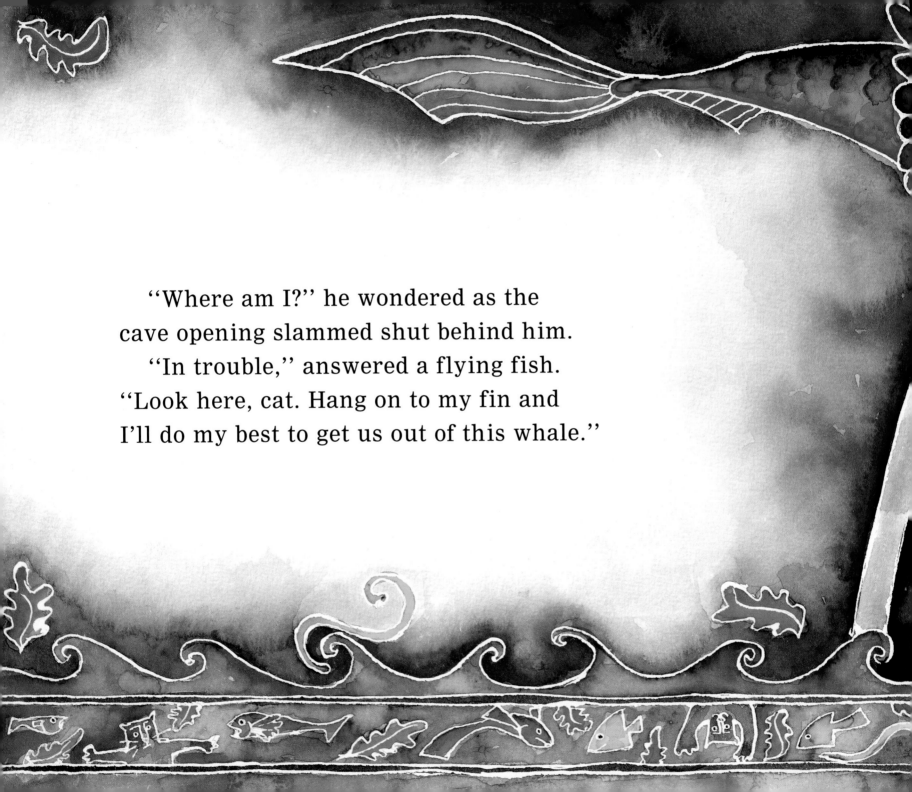

"Where am I?" he wondered as the
cave opening slammed shut behind him.
    "In trouble," answered a flying fish.
"Look here, cat. Hang on to my fin and
I'll do my best to get us out of this whale."

They made it, but Winston was exhausted.
"I'm not sure the sea is the right place for
me after all," he remarked.

"What's the matter?" asked the flying
fish. "Are you sick?"

"Yes," said Winston. "Homesick."

"Hold tight, then," bubbled the
flying fish. "I'll give you a lift."

A few moments later, Winston was back on land. He waved a soggy thank-you to the fish, then headed home, stopping only to scoop up a few feathers along the way.

That night he sat again by the fire, listening to tall, fishy tales. "I've had enough of the sea," he purred.

"But flying – now
that's the life for me!"

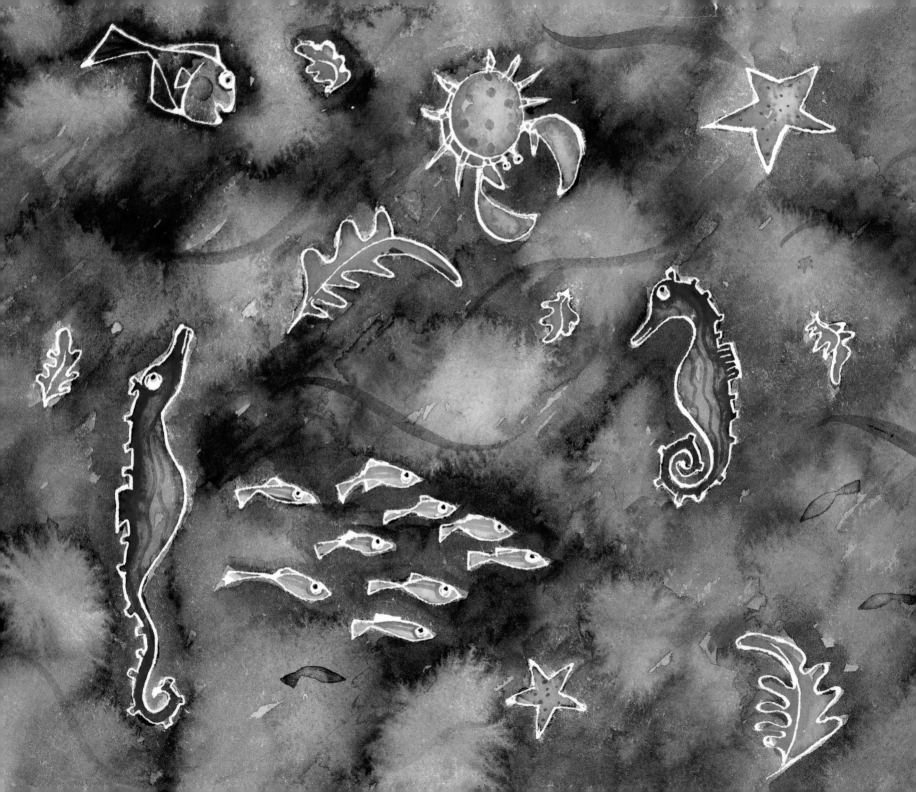